Copyright © 2020 Clavis Publishing Inc., New York

Originally published as *Oeps, ik liet de citroentaart vallen* in Belgium
and the Netherlands by Clavis Uitgeverij, 2019
English translation from the Dutch by Clavis Publishing Inc., New York

Visit us on the Web at www.clavis-publishing.com.

*Oops, I Dropped the Lemon Tart* written by An Swerts and illustrated by Eline van Lindenhuizen

ISBN 978-1-60537-579-3

This book was printed in April 2020 at Nikara, M. R. Štefánika 858/25, 963 01 Krupina, Slovakia.

First Edition
10 9 8 7 6 5 4 3 2 1

Written by An Swerts

Illustrations by Eline van Lindenhuizen

# Oops, I Dropped the Lemon Tart

Clavis

**NEW YORK**

Lucy and Evan had just finished their swim lesson.
"Who wants to jump off the diving board?"
the teacher asked the class.
"Yippee!" all the children cheered.
That is, all the children except Lucy.

The other children were surprised that Lucy didn't
want to jump off the board, but Evan wasn't.
He was Lucy's best friend and knew that she worried
about everything. She hadn't always been that way . . .

Lucy was a cheerful, happy baby from the moment she was born. Her eyes sparkled so brightly, it made everyone feel warm inside. Lucy loved to laugh and play outside. She especially loved to be with her Nonna. Lucy's father worked hard in his restaurant. But it was always fun with Nonna.

Evan lived right next door. Sometimes he would come over to play.
Then they played that they were pirates. Or lived in a castle.
Evan was so funny.
He always made Lucy laugh.

Finally the day came that Lucy and Evan got to go to school.
Oh, they couldn't wait to learn how to read and write!

The first weeks of school just flew by. The leaves on the trees were beginning to turn from lush green to warm red and yellow when Nonna noticed something. Lucy rarely talked about school, and her eyes had lost their sparkle. She was so quiet. Even Evan couldn't make her laugh.

One day, Lucy came home and burst into tears. "Oh, Nonna, everything is going wrong. I dropped *all* of my crayons in art class today. My pencil broke when we practiced writing. I'm the last one to button up my coat when it's time to go outside. And I spilled my juice during snack time."

So Nonna and Lucy went to see the teacher.
"Well, yes, Lucy makes mistakes sometimes,"
the teacher said to Nonna.
"But," she said to Lucy, "that's okay.
Everyone makes mistakes…"
As long as you try your best. And you *do*.
You have nothing to be worried about."
"Very true," Nonna said with a nod.

But Lucy didn't stop worrying.
While the other children ran fast in gym class,
Lucy just trotted along, afraid she might trip.

And while the others busied themselves with scissors at the art table,
Lucy walked away. She only answered questions in class when she really had to.
She got quieter and quieter.

Then Nonna had an idea. "Robert," she said to Lucy's dad, "why doesn't Lucy give you a hand in the kitchen."

"Would you like to help me, Lucy?" her dad asked. Lucy just nodded. She liked being in the kitchen with her dad. And she would love to feel useful. "Can Evan help too?" she asked. "Sure!" said Robert.

Every day after school, Lucy and Evan helped at the restaurant. And slowly but surely Lucy gained confidence. She felt useful.

Until one day . . . a man came to the restaurant to write a review for the newspaper.

"Lucy," her dad called. "Please bring out our famous lemon tart."

Lucy held her breath. Such an important task! She took the plate with both hands, stretched out her arms, and . . .

the plate slipped right out of her hands! The dessert fell to the floor. *Splat!*
But the plate stayed in one piece, and the lemon tart looked like a beautiful sunset.
"It looks wonderful," said Robert. "Yes!" Evan cheered. "Just like a painting!"
And do you want to know what the reviewer thought?

He thought the dessert was "dazzling" and "highly original," as he wrote in the newspaper.
"You see, Lucy," said her dad, "you don't have to be afraid to make mistakes. Making mistakes is part of life. And sometimes something beautiful comes out of a mistake."

And after that, every time Lucy got that worried
feeling again, afraid to try something new,
afraid to make mistakes, she thought
of two words: *lemon tart* . . .

and the worry went away.

*And do you want to know what happened to Lucy so many years later?*

Dear Lucy

You don't like to make mistakes.
But, you know, it's part of life.
So feel free
to dream,
and dare,
and do!

It's okay to make mistakes,
with a tear
or a laugh.
Like the teacher says:
"It only matters,
that you try your best."
And that, my dear Lucy,
is so very true.

Nonna

## INSPIRED BY A TRUE STORY

This picture book story is inspired by an incident that really happened a few years ago in Osteria Francescana, a restaurant in Modena (Italy) that was voted best restaurant in the world in 2016 and 2018.

The sous chef Taka Kondo dropped the last piece of lemon tart for that evening. Taka felt horrible and worried that the chef would be angry at him. But the chef, Massimo Bottura, cried out, surprised: "Look, Taka, how beautiful it looks, in pieces like this!" A few days later a new dessert appeared on the menu, and since then, Oops, I Dropped the Lemon Tart has been a widely acclaimed dessert. All over the world, chefs try to imitate the perfect imperfection of it.

**Taka Kondo:**

*"That day I learned
that if you embrace your mistakes
and learn something from them,
you can get ahead in life."*